Enjoy!

The Adventures of the BRAIN BROS.

BOOK #1 ATTACK OF THE VIRTUAL VIPER!

WRITTEN BY DR. MICHAEL SLONE

ILLUSTRATED BY CONNOR SNOW

DEDICATIONS

This book is dedicated to young readers everywhere, and their parents and educators, who are looking for a book with "super" heroes and (brain) powers that kids can relate to and admire, illustrations that will inspire imagination and multiple intelligences, and text that build reading and rhyming skills while introducing new vocabulary and emphasizing healthy values—values that are especially important in today's digital age. On a personal note—to my devoted wife, loving mother, and caring siblings, I can't thank each of you enough for your endless support. To my sons Patrick, Brendan and Nick (The Brain Bros.), always embrace your amazing brain powers, love one another, and help others.
Love, Michael/Dad

Once upon a time there were three brothers, birthed from the same mother but very different from one another; each with unique brains unlike any other.

Brendan is the creative creator—impressively building, drawing, measuring and engineering, constantly imagining.

Nick, so strong and nice, and cool as ice; quick to right any wrong—and never let a friend fall. Nick is a mighty mate to all!

Despite their unique brains and talents, the brothers maintained great balance; loving to try whatever, the brothers played happily with one another and all others.

The boys soon learned their friends were lured indoors by an evil pied piper:

The Virtual Viper!

This digital devil delivered devices designed to distract minds, consume time and hijack our senses!

The Virtual Viper made screens so addicting that children and teens quickly stopped talking, playing and learning.

The Virtual Viper's virus controlled kids' screens, and entered every scene, even their dreams!

The Virtual Viper targeted kids who before loved to laugh and actively play, but now passively puttered and stayed online and alone; the brothers soon moaned, "What can we do to change this tone?"

The virtual virus had taken its toll, but the brothers brainstormed a plan to save the others' souls, with a hand from their favorite teachers, Ms. England and Mr. Rolle!

Their instructors inspired the brothers to realize everyone has a super hero inside of them; a brain unlike any other, ready to train super powers and help others!

That night, like any other, the brothers had a device-free family supper, and they got this advice from both father and mother:

The brothers went to their tree house, where they brainstormed together how to unleash their talents into brain powers to save the others!

This is how they became:

The **BRAIN BROS.**

Patrick became **WORD WIZ** - coding words into spells that only he can tell!

The
BRAIN BROS.
must reverse the virus to save the universe!

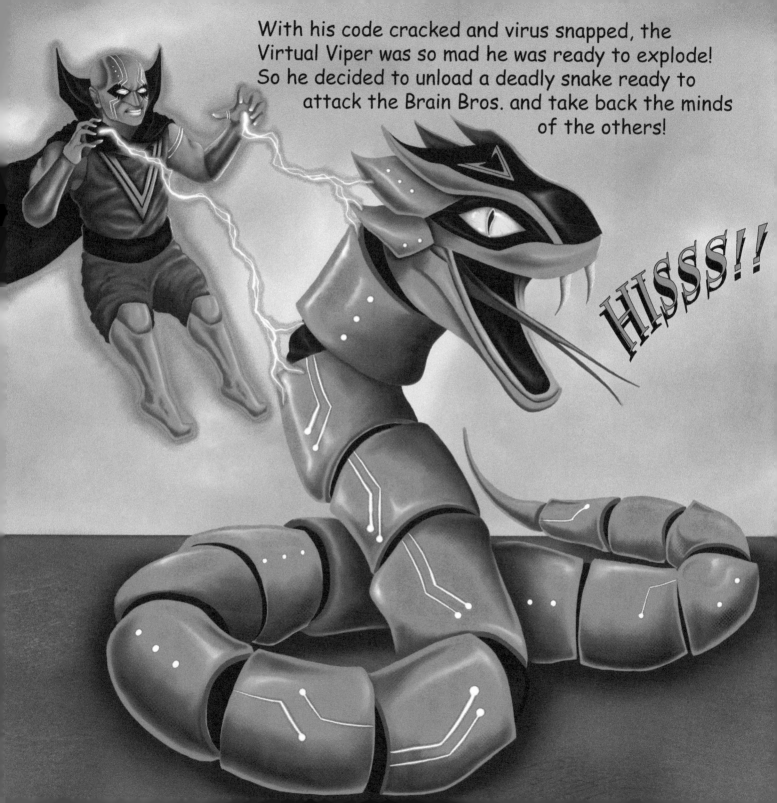

But THE CREATOR imagined, illustrated and engineered a flying fire-breathing dragon!

The dragon was able to air raid and take away the serpent—finally freeing them from the Viper's venom!!!

It was time for MIGHTY MATE,
leading with great strength,
to facilitate a group of
brave teammates!

The police were then called in, to bring peace and arrest the Viper for his sins, so his virtual virus would never win!

Everybody cheered hooray! The neighborhood returned to feeling good, and kids were free to learn, play and run all day!

Children could train their brains to do whatever they say, without a device to take their mind away.

It was truly a beautiful day!!!

THE END